SPIRIT
STALLION OF THE CIMARRON™

A Friend in Rain

P9-DNI-419

adapted by
CATHY HAPKA

DREAMWORKS®

SPIRIT
STALLION OF THE CIMARRON ™

PUFFIN BOOKS

Published by the Penguin Group

Penguin Putnam Books for Young Readers,

345 Hudson Street, New York, New York 10014, U.S.A.

Penguin Books Ltd, 80 Strand, London WC2R ORL, England

Penguin Books Australia Ltd, Ringwood, Victoria, Australia

Penguin Books Canada Ltd, 10 Alcorn Avenue, Toronto, Ontario, Canada M4V 3B2

Penguin Books (N.Z.) Ltd, 182-190 Wairau Road, Auckland 10, New Zealand

Penguin Books Ltd, Registered Offices: Harmondsworth, Middlesex, England

Published by Puffin Books, a division of Penguin Putnam Books for Young Readers, 2002

1 3 5 7 9 10 8 6 4 2

CONTENTS

Chapter One
Homeland

*S*pirit was born on the open plains of the American West. He spent his days racing with the eagle and running like the wind. Like his father before him, the strong buckskin stallion became the leader of the Cimarron herd.

One day, a group of wranglers came to Spirit's Homeland. They captured the noble mustang and took him away from his herd. That was the day Spirit learned that there was another world on the far side of the Red Mesa....

A wrangler named Bill brought Spirit to the cavalry

fort—though Spirit resisted him all the way. The man
sold the stubborn stallion to the soldiers there.

"The army just bought a fine animal, Sergeant," Bill
said.

Spirit couldn't understand the man's words. He was
confused and angry—the wranglers had taken him from
his herd, his Homeland, and everything else he had ever
known.

Although he was roped, Spirit reared up on his hind
legs, trying to escape. He looked around the fort wildly.
Nearby, a group of horses was standing quietly in a line.
These horses were not grazing or resting or playing like
the horses Spirit knew. Their heads were up and they
were staring forward. They wore strange objects on their
backs, and odd straps banded their noses and ears.
Strangest of all, humans were sitting on their backs!

What was wrong with these horses? Spirit wondered in horror as he reared again. How could they allow another creature to sit upon them like that, like a cougar leaping onto the back of its prey?

Spirit stared at one of the horses. The horse gazed back and snorted sympathetically, taking a step toward Spirit. The human on its back yanked at the straps wrapped around its head. The horse stepped back into line.

Spirit flattened his ears. He glanced around, frightened. Like all horses, Spirit had been born to run. On the open plains, predators could come from anywhere. A swift set of legs was the only protection a horse had.

And now Spirit was in this strange human place, surrounded by things and creatures he didn't understand. Panic grew in his heart, forming one strong message: RUN!

He bolted, dragging one of the humans behind him. BANG!

Spirit skidded to a halt, nostrils flared. What was that? It had sounded like a clap of thunder. But there was no sign of storm clouds overhead. Could the humans have made that terrifying sound?

Straight ahead, a new horse had appeared. Sitting atop this horse was another human—the Colonel. His face was intelligent yet stern.

"What seems to be the problem, gentlemen?" the Colonel asked his soldiers.

"We got us a crazy one here, Sir," one of them replied.

Another nodded. "Pure mustang, Colonel."

The Colonel came forward to look at Spirit. "The Army has dealt with wild horses before." He lifted Spirit's mane with his riding crop to get a better look at his face.

Spirit flattened his ears in anger. He didn't like having a human so close. Since he couldn't get away—the men were holding him too tightly—he grabbed the Colonel's crop and bit it.

The Colonel chuckled. "Train this animal, Sergeant," he ordered before turning away.

Spirit was hauled deeper into the fort. The black-

smith tried to shoe and brand him. But Spirit fought against him. He might be trapped in the humans' strange homeland, but he would not let them nail metal shoes to his feet or brand his shoulder with a red-hot iron.

Finally the humans gave up and dragged Spirit to the corral. Spirit tensed. He guessed what was coming—he had seen the humans atop other horses coming from this area of the fort.

But he wasn't like those other horses. No human would ever sit on him!

The men shouted as they herded Spirit into a small pen and strapped a saddle to his back. Spirit tried to fight them, but it was no use. A soldier climbed carefully onto his back.

"*Heeaa!*" he cried as the others opened the gate.

Spirit launched himself out of the pen, kicking and bucking. He could no longer see the human on his back. All he could feel was the rider's weight—just as he had felt the weight of a cougar that he had once fought. He had escaped from the cougar by throwing it off of his back. He could escape this man in the same way!

Seconds later the man hit the ground. Spirit tossed his head and snorted. Perhaps he had taught the two-legged a lesson. Spirit looked around at the other horses, who whinnied in approval. They seemed to enjoy the show.

But the humans had not learned. Another soldier tried to ride Spirit, and another. Spirit bucked off every one of them. The Colonel watched it all.

After Spirit threw the last soldier, he charged over to the Colonel. He snorted, staring down the human leader.

Spirit had proved that no man could ride him. Now the Colonel would have to let him go.

But the Colonel didn't back down. He stared back, his gaze stern and even. For a moment man and horse stood face-to-face, glaring at each other.

Finally the Colonel spoke to his men. "Tie this horse to the post," he said coldly. "No food or water. Three days."

Chapter Two
A Narrow Escape

Spirit tried over and over to break free. But the post was not weak like the humans. It remained steadfast no matter how hard he pulled.

The other horses watched from the stables. They felt sorry for Spirit. They knew he didn't belong here, with the two-leggeds. He belonged where he'd been born, running free across the open plains of his Homeland.

Night arrived, and Spirit gazed up at the stars. He saw the brightest star in the sky, the one he'd often seen from his Homeland. He thought of his herd and wondered if they missed him as much as he missed them.

The next day, Spirit was still trying to break free from the post. He was hot and thirsty and tired, but he was determined not to give up.

Suddenly he heard shouting. Spirit looked up and saw a young human being brought forward by the soldiers. Spirit looked at the new human curiously. He was

almost as tall as the soldiers, but Spirit could tell that he was not quite a man yet. His hair was dark and long, and he wore soft deerskin leggings. His face was stubborn and angry.

"What do we have here?" the Colonel asked.

"We caught him by the supply wagons, Sir," a soldier replied.

The Colonel approached the boy and looked him over. "Ah," he said thoughtfully. "A Lakota. Take him to the post."

The soldiers brought the boy over and tied him near Spirit.

The young human, Little Creek, stared at the horse. His face softened, and he almost smiled. Spirit stared back.

Then Little Creek clucked, startling Spirit. The

horse snorted. The boy snorted back.

Spirit wasn't sure what to make of this human. He turned away, ready to kick if necessary. But the boy remained quiet and didn't threaten Spirit, so Spirit just kept an eye on him for the rest of the day.

That night just before the dawn, Spirit took a break from his struggle to escape. Suddenly he heard Little Creek make a noise. It sounded like the hoot of the owls that Spirit had often heard swooping over his Homeland.

Moments later, a howl responded from outside the fort. Then a knife came flying over the wall and landed at the boy's feet.

Spirit cocked a curious ear as he watched what was going on. There was no end to the strange ways of the two-leggeds.

Little Creek grabbed the knife. But before he could

cut his ropes, soldiers came pouring out of the fort.

It was time for the Colonel to try to ride Spirit.

Once again, the men cinched the saddle to Spirit's back. Once again, he struggled in the pen as a human climbed atop him. And once again, as the gate opened, he lunged forward and began to leap and whirl.

This time, though, the human stayed put. No matter what Spirit did, he could not dislodge the Colonel from the saddle.

Spirit fought harder. He fought the weight on his back, and the pressure of the metal bit in his mouth. But it was no good. The Colonel rode through every buck and kick.

"You see, gentlemen," the Colonel said as Spirit came to a halt. "*Any* horse can be broken."

Breathing hard, Spirit glanced around. He saw the

other horses watching. He saw the young Lakota watching. He could tell that they all thought he was beaten. But he was not ready to admit defeat.

Gathering his strength, Spirit swung his head, yanking the reins from the Colonel's hands. Then he began twisting and leaping against the fence. The cinch of the saddle scraped the rails and broke. The Colonel—and the saddle—flew off his back at last.

Little Creek stared at Spirit in amazement. The other horses reared up, excited by Spirit's triumph. Their riders shouted and tried to bring their mounts back under control, but for once the cavalry horses ignored them.

"Soldier!" the Colonel shouted at one of his men. "Secure that horse!"

Suddenly Little Creek broke free of his ropes. He had cut them with his knife while the soldiers were watching Spirit.

He raced straight for Spirit. The stallion was surprised when the young human grabbed for his neck and mane, but he didn't bother to fight him. He could only think of escaping from the fort.

He took off, racing out of the corral. Little Creek hung on for dear life, his legs flying out behind him as Spirit ran.

Spirit crashed through a group of cavalry horses tied to a post, freeing them. They followed, snorting and whinnying, as he raced for the gate. Moments later Spirit and the other horses galloped out of the fort and onto the open land before them.

Freedom! Spirit ran like the wind. He hardly noticed the Lakota boy still clinging to his neck. Freedom at last!

CHAPTER THREE
A New Friend

Spirit was still running
when another horse
appeared out of nowhere. He
looked over and saw that it
was a brown-and-white pinto
mare. The wind blew her
long, silky mane as she ran
alongside Spirit.

Little Creek finally let go
of Spirit's neck. He turned and
leaped onto the mare's back,
calling out her name, Rain, as
he jumped.

Spirit blinked in surprise.
Instead of bucking off the
human, the mare seemed
content to let him stay on her
back. Spirit's gallop slowed as

he watched the curious sight. Rain kept pace with him for a moment, the boy urging her on with his legs.

Then she swung around, her body blocking Spirit so that he had to stop. She gazed at Spirit curiously. Spirit raised his head and gazed back. She was the most beautiful mare he had ever seen. But why had she stopped? Was she playing?

Rain was curious about Spirit, too. Who was this bold young stallion? Where had Little Creek found him?

Suddenly two more horses appeared. More young humans were riding on their bare backs. The boys tossed ropes around Spirit's neck and shoulders.

Spirit shook his head, trying to escape. But it was no use. He couldn't believe it. One moment he was free. The next—trapped again!

Rain watched as Spirit struggled. She wondered why he resisted. Couldn't he see that these humans wanted to be his friends?

Spirit had no choice but to follow Little Creek and the others to their village. Would they try to ride him as the other humans had done? He didn't know. But he knew that whatever they did, he would never give in. The humans might be able to control his body, but his heart would be proud and free—forever.

At the Lakota camp, Little Creek led Spirit into a

corral. Spirit snorted suspiciously as the boy moved
toward his head.

"Steady . . . easy . . ." the boy murmured. "I'm not
going to hurt you."

Spirit stood his ground as Little Creek reached for
the cavalry bridle—and pulled it off.

Spirit was surprised at the boy's kindness as Little
Creek removed the strange straps and tended to his
wounds. But he still didn't trust the young human. He
was still fenced in. He snorted and moved off, testing
the boundaries of the corral as Little Creek slipped away.

He saw Rain watching him from nearby. The pinto
mare was not fenced in. Yet she did not run away. Why?
Spirit didn't understand. Why would a horse willingly
stay with humans? Why would a horse allow a human to

ride on her back? Rain was beautiful, but strange. She was nothing like the mares in Spirit's herd back in his Homeland.

Spirit was tired after his long, difficult adventure. Even though he had no one to watch over him as he slept, he had to rest. Otherwise he would be too tired to figure out a way to escape.

He awoke a short while later. To his surprise, there was a pile of tasty apples nearby. Where had they come from?

Climbing to his feet, Spirit sniffed at the apples and then began to eat. A quick movement from outside the corral caught his eye. He raised his head and saw Rain watching him curiously.

Spirit snorted and moved toward her. Rain tossed her head shyly. Spirit pranced, demanding her attention.

The pinto mare might be strange. But he was sure she would come to him when he called her. After all, he was a lead stallion.

A human cry interrupted the horses. Rain pricked her ears as Little Creek called her name again. Spirit watched in amazement as the pretty mare turned and trotted toward the human.

Rain nickered as she approached Little Creek. The human boy greeted her with a pat and a scratch. She nibbled at the boy's hair and snorted in his face. He laughed and tugged gently at her mane. Spirit noticed that Little Creek had placed a long eagle's feather in her silky mane.

Spirit just couldn't understand the other horse's behavior. She was treating the scrawny two-legged

human like one of their own kind! It was downright
unnatural.

Little Creek entered the corral and carefully
approached the stallion.

"Great Mustang, today I will ride you," the boy said
solemnly.

Spirit cocked a curious ear. What was the boy up to now?

Little Creek came toward him with a blanket. Spirit
stepped away, keeping a wary eye on the strange fabric
as it flapped in the breeze.

Nearby, Rain lifted her head from her grazing. She
watched as Little Creek moved forward again. Again,
Spirit skipped out of the way.

Little Creek chased after Spirit and tried to fling the
blanket onto his back. The stallion darted out of range,
snorting with annoyance.

Rain shook her head as she watched. Why did Spirit fight? Little Creek would never hurt him. But the new-comer didn't seem to understand that. Instead, he danced away as Little Creek approached again.

The game went on a little longer. Finally Spirit had had enough. Letting out a noisy snort, he whirled—and charged straight at the boy. Little Creek dropped the blanket and ran, vaulting over the fence just in time. Spirit stopped and watched, amused.

But Rain didn't find it funny. She was angry—how dare he treat Little Creek that way? She raced up to Spirit and let out a fierce cry.

Spirit took a step backward, surprised and perplexed. Why was the mare so angry? He had only been defending himself against the human. He had done nothing wrong. She was the one who let the human ride on her

back. She was the one who stayed near the village when she could easily run away.

Spirit backed away meekly as she scolded him. He might be leader of the herd—but he knew better than to mess with an angry mare.

A while later Little Creek entered the corral again. This time he brought Rain with him.

"Okay, Rain," he said to the pinto. "Let's see if you can teach this mustang some manners."

Rain stood patiently while Little Creek looped a tether around her neck, then put the other end around Spirit's neck. She understood that she was to teach the young stallion what Little Creek couldn't—how to behave.

Spirit didn't realize what was happening until he was

already tethered to the mare. For a second, he was confused. Then he noticed that Little Creek was standing near the corral gate, which was wide open. The boy gestured to the opening.

Freedom! Spirit's ears pricked, and his heart raced.

He lunged for the gate, racing out of the corral. But the rope brought him up short.

Snorting and glancing around, he saw Rain with her feet planted and her ears back. What was the strange mare doing now? This was their chance to escape and run free! Why didn't she follow him?

Rain sat down stubbornly and dug her hooves in as Spirit tugged at the tether. She would show this stallion who was boss around here.

She got up slowly and began to lead Spirit toward the village. Spirit shook his head, trying to loosen the tether. He planted his own feet, refusing to be

led toward the human dwellings.

Rain stopped and glared at him. Then she had another idea. She took a few steps toward him.

For a moment, Spirit thought she was giving in. She wanted to run with him after all!

Instead, she stepped around him, smiling at him coyly. He watched her. He didn't notice that Rain had wrapped the tether around his legs. Around . . . around . . . around . . . and . . .

THUD!

OOOF!

The stallion landed on his side in the dust as the mare pulled the tether taut, yanking his legs out from under him. He blinked in surprise, trying to regain his breath as Rain looked at him with a sparkle in her eye.

Rain was no ordinary mare. That much was certain. She wasn't afraid to stand up to Spirit, to show him what she thought. He had never met another horse like her.

Spirit climbed to his feet. The mare watched cautiously. Spirit bowed his head and snorted.

Rain had won his respect. From now on, the two of them were herdmates—friends.

CHAPTER FOUR
Rain's Village

Spirit followed as his new friend Rain led him back toward the village. He had no choice—they were still tied together. But now he didn't mind following.

As they entered the village, new sights and smells met Spirit at every step. Humans ran in and out of their dwellings, talking and laughing. Many of them stopped to watch the handsome new stallion go by.

It was all very unfamiliar to Spirit, just as the cavalry fort had been. But it was more peaceful here. The humans seemed kinder, and the animals content.

Small children played outside some of the teepees. A tiny girl spotted the horses coming. She toddled straight toward them, smiling and burbling.

Spirit jumped back, eyeing the odd little creature suspiciously. Beside him, Rain was amused.

The youngster came closer, gurgling and stumbling on her unsteady legs. "Horsie!" she cried happily, waving her arms.

Rain lowered her head toward the child. Cautiously, Spirit slowly lowered his head beside hers, keeping a close eye on the small human.

The child giggled. She stretched up—and grabbed Spirit's nose. He snorted in surprise. The girl fell back on the ground and started crying. Spirit looked at Rain in confusion. What was wrong? Had he hurt it?

He lowered his head again and sniffed at the girl. She reached up and took hold of his muzzle. Spirit raised his head in surprise and lifted the little human,

her feet swinging free from the ground. Then he gently
lowered her back down.

She giggled. "Bye-bye, Horsie!" Then she let go and
waved to Spirit and Rain as she toddled off.

Hiding her amusement, Rain led Spirit toward Little
Creek and his friends. The young braves were drawing
strange shapes on their horses with blue paint. One of
the young braves drew a blue circle around a horse's eye.
Spirit was surprised to see the other horses stand so still
as they were painted.

Little Creek reached to draw a shape on Spirit,
but Spirit would not let himself be painted! He
kicked over the bowl of blue paint, splashing it all
over Little Creek. Spirit snorted, amused at the sight
But Little Creek was not angry. Instead, he surprised
Spirit again by laughing good-naturedly. Confused,

pirit cocked his head at Rain. He would never understand these two-leggeds.

Rain showed Spirit the rest of the village, then led him to the land outside. A clear, rocky river meandered across the grassy sweep of the valley. A short distance away, the water widened out into a shallow lagoon. Overlooking it all, a craggy ridge was outlined against the blue sky.

The horses stopped beneath an apple tree heavy with fruit. Rain looked longingly at a juicy red apple hanging just out of her reach. Spirit saw her glance. Suddenly he wanted to take care of her, the way he took care of his herd back home.

He gathered his strength and sprang up into the air, grabbing for the apple. He landed a second later with the prize in his teeth.

He offered the apple to Rain, who accepted the gift shyly.

Next, Rain led Spirit to the lagoon. The cool water felt good on Spirit's dusty, tired legs as he sloshed in after her. The two of them spent a long time wading and swimming among the lily pads in the shallow water.

Spirit was amazed at how special this mare was. He thought of his Homeland. His heart ached, missing his old life with his herd. But Rain had showed him that this new life with the humans didn't have to be bad. What more did she have to teach him?

Later, Spirit and Rain watched an eagle soar far overhead. Watching the eagle fly, Spirit longed to fly with it—to return to his Homeland. But for the first time, something held him back. He didn't want to leave Rain.

As the days passed, Little Creek tried again and again
to ride Spirit. After a while Spirit hardly minded the
boy's attempts. Each time, he would let Little Creek get
a little closer.

First he let him put a hand on his shoulder before
running off.

The next time, he allowed Little Creek to lift the
blanket.

Then he permitted the boy to lay the blanket across
his back and withers.

Finally he waited until the boy had jumped onto his
back before taking off across the corral, bucking him off
within a few strides.

Spirit had to hand it to the boy. Little Creek wouldn't
give up.

Rain watched their antics from nearby. She was amused, though she couldn't understand why Spirit was still being so stubborn. She didn't mind when Little Creek rode her. He was her friend.

Little Creek's friends often watched, too. One day, they laughed loudly as Spirit dumped the boy onto the dusty ground yet again.

Rain snorted, dismayed at the embarrassed look on Little Creek's face.

Spirit put his ears back. He didn't like to see Rain upset, and he wanted to show her that he had also come to care for Little Creek. He snorted, pawed the ground, and charged at the fence where the other boys were sitting. They let out shrieks of terror, tumbling from the fence and running away.

When the other boys were gone, Spirit snorted with satisfaction. He looked around for Rain, but he didn't see her. Then he turned back and walked over to Little Creek. He put his muzzle against the boy's hand, wanting to let him know he was safe.

Little Creek stroked him gently. "I'm never going to ride you, am I?" he said softly. He paused, looking at the noble mustang and thinking hard. "And no one ever should," he added at last.

Spirit didn't understand the boy's words, but he could tell that Little Creek was struggling to come to a decision. He watched as the boy stood and draped the blanket over the fence post. Then he walked over to the corral gate.

Spirit snorted uncertainly as Little Creek opened the gate and motioned toward him.

"You can go," Little Creek said. "It's okay. Go!"

Spirit wasn't sure what to make of this. Was it a new game? He cocked one ear toward the opening and the other toward Little Creek, wondering what to do.

Little Creek hurried toward him, shooing him through the opening. "Go on—get out of here!" he cried. "Go home." Spirit finally galloped freely through the gate of the corral.

Spirit found Rain near the apple tree. As soon as she saw him, she understood what had happened. Spirit tried to convince her to come with him—to run free at his side across the plains to his Homeland. More than

anything, he wanted to share it all with her.

Rain was uncertain. She was safe and happy in her life with Little Creek. But she couldn't imagine never seeing Spirit again.

Before she could decide what to do, her sensitive ears picked up sharp sounds—like gunshots—coming from across the valley. Spirit heard them, too.

Moments later, the cavalry swarmed into the valley with the Colonel in the lead!

CHAPTER FIVE
The River

Rain raced toward the village before Spirit could stop her. She wanted to help her friend, Little Creek.

Spirit ran after her, reaching the village just as the Colonel's forces invaded. Horses and people were everywhere. In the noise and confusion, Spirit lost sight of Rain.

He whinnied frantically, calling to her. A moment later, she burst back into view. Her nostrils were flared, and her eyes were angry. Little Creek was on her back, whooping loudly at the invaders.

The Colonel rode near the river, chasing after some frightened villagers who were running into the water for safety. Rain and Little Creek spotted him—and charged.

The Colonel spurred his horse toward the boy and mare, raising his arm. Spirit paused for a moment, glancing at Little Creek and Rain. He didn't really understand the thing that the Colonel was pointing at the boy, but he could tell that the Colonel meant to harm Rain and Little Creek.

Suddenly, Spirit heard a loud crack! Spirit saw Rain stumble and fall into the river, throwing Little Creek off her back as she tumbled.

Spirit whinnied anxiously, running toward the fallen mare. As he neared the river, he saw that Little Creek had fallen into the racing river as well. And the Colonel was again pointing his weapon at Little Creek.

Spirit knew that Rain would want him to help her friend. He knew what he had to do. Veering toward the riverbank, he rammed into the Colonel's horse with all his might, knocking the man from the saddle.

The Colonel shouted in surprise and anger as he tumbled to the ground. Little Creek could hardly believe what had just happened. The stubborn mustang, the stallion who refused to let anyone ride him, had just saved his life. He would not forget it.

Meanwhile Spirit was galloping toward Rain. But the current was carrying her downstream. Spirit jumped into the cold water and started swimming after her.

Finally Spirit caught up to Rain. She was tired and hurt, but now he could help her out of the swift river. Spirit swam close, and Rain leaned on Spirit's back. Slowly Spirit pulled her toward the riverbank. The

current was strong, but Spirit was determined to over-
come it and get them both to safety. But then he heard
an odd rushing noise. It was a waterfall—and the river
was carrying them toward it!

Spirit fought the current desperately, but could not
reach the bank in time. The roar of the water grew louder
and louder as it swept the horses over the falls.

Spirit fell and fell, then plunged into the deep pool
below the falls. He swam to the surface and looked
around. Where was Rain? He spotted her lying on the
bank and swam to her. She was hurt, but she was still
breathing.

Spirit moved close, trying to help her, but suddenly,

more soldiers appeared. They shouted, tossing a rope over his neck. Spirit struggled, but the ropes held tight. He was captured again!

He fought and snorted as the men dragged him away. He whinnied to Rain, and she lifted her head to answer. He had to get back to her, to make sure she was all right!

But he couldn't. The soldiers were too strong. Spirit's head sagged hopelessly as they led him away. Would he ever see Rain again?

CHAPTER SIX
Rail Town

Spirit hardly noticed as the men led him toward a train, a giant metal monster like nothing he had ever seen before. The men loaded him onto the train along with some other horses they had captured from the village.

Soon the train was chugging across the plains and into the mountains. Snow began to fall, slowly at first and then faster. The other horses nickered to him, but Spirit didn't answer. He felt helpless and despondent.

Where were they going? Spirit had no idea. But as he looked at the swirling snow,

he thought about his mother and his herd and he felt his
spirits lift. He knew that wherever he ended up, he had
to stay strong—for his herd and for Rain. She had
taught him so much. He couldn't give up now. As long as
he was alive, he would continue to fight for his freedom.
Spirit lifted his head, and whinnied to the other horses.

Finally the train wheezed to a stop at a rail town in
the mountains. As the humans unloaded the horses, the
scene that greeted Spirit was even stranger and more
frightening than the cavalry fort. Here, the humans had
destroyed the land itself. Great swaths of fallen trees and
crumbled rock stretched as far as his eyes could see. Hot,
smoky, foreign smells met his flared nostrils. The loud
KA-BLOOM! of a dynamite blast erupted in the distance,
assaulting his ears.

Spirit had been brought to the rail town to help

build a new railroad. Soon he was chained together with dozens of other horses. They were to pull a heavy train engine on a sled over the mountain.

The horses strained against their harnesses, and the sled slowly began to climb up the steep slope. They worked all day, and by evening, the team had almost reached the top of the mountain. Spirit was near the front, and was one of the first to look out over the plains below. Beyond them, he saw a familiar outline of peaks and crags. His heart pounded as he realized he was looking toward the mountains of his Homeland. They were just a few miles away!

Suddenly he realized what that meant. The men wanted to run their train line right through Spirit's Homeland! That was the moment when Spirit knew he had to stop pulling—and start fighting as he'd never fought before.

But how could he fight while he was trapped in the humans' chains?

If only Rain were here. She could always find a way to get what she wanted—like the time she'd tightened the tether around Spirit's legs. . . .

That gave him an idea. Letting out a cry, Spirit fell to the ground.

Several workers rushed toward him, thinking he was injured or sick. They unhitched him and dragged him off to the side.

Spirit didn't wait for another chance. Leaping to his feet, he raced toward the sled. As the men shouted and chased him, they tossed a chain around his neck. But Spirit was still able to release one team of horses, then another.

Once all the horses were free, the engine started to

lide back down the steep slope. Spirit raced ahead of it, he chain still dangling from his neck. A moment later, he locomotive crashed into a building, then slammed nto another train engine.

KA-BLAM!

The explosion was even louder than the dynamite. Fire shot out from the blast, setting nearby trees alight.

Spirit galloped into the woods. He had escaped from he engine, but now an even deadlier enemy was chasing him—fire. Smoke filled his lungs. He had to reach the iver. There, he would be safe.

The mustang was faster than most other creatures, but the fire was faster still. A monstrous wall of flame was roaring up behind Spirit. He ran harder—as hard as he'd ever run—but still it gained on him.

The river. He had to reach the river!

Gasping in the smoke, Spirit saw that the only thing in his way was a large fallen tree. Just beyond, a cliff dropped off over the broad, slow-moving river.

Spirit steadied his stride as he neared the fallen tree. Gathering his strength, he launched himself into the air, clearing the obstacle easily.

But he had forgotten one thing—the chain that was still dangling from around his neck.

SNAP! The chain caught on the log and held. Spirit's head jerked, and he landed hard on the ground beside the log.

The wall of fire was still coming fast. Spirit tried to clamber to his feet, to pull the chain free. But it was caught tight at the base of a heavy branch.

Suddenly a figure appeared in the haze. A familiar human figure. It swung a hatchet, releasing the chain in one quick motion.

Little Creek! Spirit hardly had time to thank him before Little Creek grabbed Spirit and led him in a mad dash away from the fire.

CHAPTER SEVEN
Reunited

The two did not make it far before they came to the edge of a cliff and the river below. With only a moment's hesitation, Spirit and Little Creek took the desperate leap into the river below.

They hung in midair for a moment, then splashed into the water. Swimming hard, Spirit and Little Creek crossed to the other side of the river, and pulled themselves up onto the bank. Exhausted, they collapsed into a deep sleep.

The next morning, Spirit awoke and found a pile of apples nearby. He looked around and saw Little Creek on the bank, drinking from the river. Spirit had no idea how Rain's human friend had found him, but he had never been happier to see anyone in his life.

Carefully Spirit sneaked up behind Little Creek and playfully shoved him into the water. Little Creek came

p splashing, and ran at Spirit, the two leaping and
parring. Spirit knew the boy was playing with him—
his was how Little Creek used to play with Rain.
Happy, they splashed around in the water.

"I knew I would find you," Little Creek told Spirit.
He raised his hand to touch him.

But suddenly Spirit lifted his head. He heard the
sound of men and horses approaching.

It was the Colonel and his men! Little Creek
recognized them, too. His face grew dark with worry.
They started to run, but Little Creek stumbled and fell
to the ground. "Go!" he urged Spirit as the soldiers galloped down toward them. "Get out of here!"

Spirit took a few steps, but he couldn't leave Little
Creek behind. Rain wouldn't want him to. And he
didn't want to, either.

Spirit ran back to Little Creek and scooped the boy

onto his back. Little Creek grabbed him by the neck, but Spirit nudged the boy, shoving him onto his back so Little Creek could ride. It felt odd to have someone riding him, but in his heart, Spirit knew it was the right thing to do.

Spirit was still tired from pulling the train and escaping from the fire. He charged forward, with Little Creek holding on for dear life. But the cavalry men still gained on him.

The mustang ran as fast as he could. Little Creek clung to his back like a burr and did his best to stop the men racing behind them. Ahead, Spirit spotted a canyon. He raced into it with the cavalry in hot pursuit. Spirit thundered through the canyon, then veered off and galloped up a mesa, trying to lose his pursuers.

But when he reached the top, he realized he had made a terrible mistake.

They were trapped above a deep gorge!

"There they are!" one soldier shouted. "Up there!"

"Oh, no," Little Creek whispered, realizing that there was nowhere to run.

Spirit ran wildly to the far edge of the cliff. He skidded to a stop just inches from the edge. Below, he spotted the familiar form of the Colonel.

He snorted. No matter what happened now, he

ouldn't give up. He couldn't allow the humans to capture
im. Not again. He was determined to be free—no
matter what it took.

His nostrils flaring, Spirit looked across the deep,
ide gorge. He felt Little Creek's legs tighten their grip.
His new human friend knew what he was thinking. He
was willing to take the risk, too.

Spirit trotted back toward the back of the mesa. He
awed at the ground and took a deep breath. Then he
roke into a gallop—heading straight toward the edge
f the cliff.

Below, the Colonel's eyes widened as he saw them
ome into view. He could hardly believe what he was
eing. Was the stallion crazy? He would never make it. . . .

Spirit picked up speed. He felt Little Creek holding

tightly to his mane, heard him chanting a prayer. They were three strides from the edge. Two strides. One . . .

Calling on all his strength, Spirit kicked his legs hard and leaped out over the chasm. For a long second, he hung in the air, flying like his childhood friend the eagle. Rain's pretty face flashed into his mind. Little Creek lifted his arms to the sky and whooped.

Then he arced downward. His hooves scrabbled for a hold on the dusty ground and he tumbled onto the second mesa.

They had made it!

Across the ravine, the Colonel gazed at the pair in admiration. The fiery mustang was truly unique. He had risked everything to be free.

Nearby, a soldier raised his rifle and took aim. The Colonel reached out and pulled down the man's rifle.

pirit had proven himself—he had earned his freedom. He deserved to live wild and untamed, just as he'd been born.

Spirit saw the Colonel watching him. The two of them locked eyes for a moment.

The man nodded. Spirit understood the gesture. He had won the Colonel's respect. The soldiers would not be chasing him anymore.

As the cavalry retreated, Little Creek and Spirit leaped and celebrated together. They were alive, they were free—and they were going to stay that way!

Finally Spirit turned toward Little Creek, offering his back. Little Creek hesitated at first, but the stallion insisted. The boy had earned the right to ride. He was Spirit's herdmate now—his friend.

The boy vaulted onto Spirit's back, and together they headed toward Little Creek's village.

CHAPTER EIGHT
Friends Forever

When they neared the village, Little Creek slid down and gave a sharp whistle. A moment later, Rain appeared.

She raced toward Spirit. He whinnied with delight and galloped toward her. The two horses came together, rearing up in their excitement. Spirit was so happy to see her that he could hardly contain his joy.

He nuzzled her neck, knowing that he could never stand to be parted from her again. Not even if it meant staying with the humans. Even if it meant never seeing his Homeland again. He knew now that life with these humans wouldn't be so bad. She had taught him that. If she wanted him to, he would stay in the village.

But maybe there was another way. Maybe Rain would come with him, live with him in his Homeland. He gazed at her. She looked back uncertainly.

Could she do it? She wanted to be with Spirit. She had missed him every moment he was gone. She had always been happy in the village, but she was willing to give up her life with the Lakota to be with Spirit.

At that moment, Little Creek came forward. He smiled, though his eyes were full of sadness.

"You will be in my heart always," he told Rain softly. Then he turned to Spirit. "Take care of her, Spirit-Who-Could-Not-Be-Broken. I'll miss you, my friend."

He threw his arms around Spirit's neck, hugging him ght. Spirit stood for a moment. He thought about the rst time he met Little Creek so long ago. He never would ave guessed that a human would win his respect—his ve. But Little Creek had earned it. Spirit would never rget him.

As the boy loosened his grip, the stallion backed way and allowed Rain to say good-bye. Little Creek ached over and gently removed the feather from Rain's ane. Rain knew what this meant. She was free now, o. Little Creek no longer claimed her as his.

Rain looked back at Spirit and nodded. It was time r them to go.

Spirit had been waiting for so long to run free. And ow he rejoiced as he and Rain galloped across the

plains toward his Homeland. The stallion's joy grew as they passed through the familiar mountains, river, and landscapes of the plains. He couldn't wait to share it all with Rain, the way she had shared her world with him. He knew that it had been hard for her to say good-bye to her life with Little Creek. But he would do everything he could to make sure she was never sorry about her choice.

Soon the two of them would be back with his herd, where they belonged. Together, as they belonged.

And their spirits would never be broken.